SASHA'S WHITE ELEPHANT

My Dolly

Woody Guthrie

My

Dolly

Candlewick Press
Cambridge, Massachusetts

pictures by Vladimir Radunsky

I put my dolly's dress on,

I put my dolly's pants on,

I put my dolly's hat on, and she looks like this.

I put my dolly's stockings on,

I put my dolly's shoes on,

She acts just like a clown-o, and she looks like this.

Oh well, she looks like this, O.
Oh well, she looks like this, O.

Tra-la-la-la-

And she looks like this.

la-la-la,

My dolly walks for me, me,

My dolly talks for me, me,

When dolly walks and talks, and oh, she looks like this.

My dolly she can sing, sing,

My dolly she can dance, dance,

When dolly sings and dances, oh, she looks like this.

Chorus

Oh well, she looks like this, O.
Oh well, she looks like this, O.

Tra-la-la-la-la-la-lo,
And she looks like this.

Dolly says, "I want to eat, eat,"

Dolly says, "I want to drink, drink,"

When dolly eats and drinks, oh well, she looks like this.

Dolly plays with all the toys, toys,

Dolly plays with the girls and boys, boys,

When dolly runs and skips, oh well, she looks like this.

Oh well, she looks like this, O.
Oh well, she looks like this, O.

Tra-la-la-la-la-la-lo,
And she looks like this.

I know my dolly likes me,

I know my dolly loves me,

When dolly hugs and kisses me, oh, we look like this.

My dolly's getting tired now,

My dolly wants to lie down,

When dolly goes to sleep, oh well, she looks like this.

Oh well, she looks like this, O.

WILL'S TURTLE

WYLIE'S LION

ANNA'S RED CAT

Oh well, she looks like this, O.

VLADIMIR'S LADY ELEPHANT.

Tra-la-la-la - la-la-la,
And she looks like
this.

PETR'S BIRDS

VLADIMIR'S BALDY DOLLY

To all the little dollies who dressed up in
hats and scarfs and danced to this song for
25 years at the Marjorie Mazia School of Dance in
Sheepshead Bay, Brooklyn (1951–1976). —N. G.

Thank you, Lucy Dresnin.
Thank you, Marin Gang and Sabine Gang.
Thank you, Wylie Leabo.
Thank you, Blake McCartney and Will McCartney.
Thank you, Raffi Pontes and Remy Pontes.
Thank you, Nathaniel Santoro.
Thank you, Petr Spina.
Thank you, Alexander (Zippy) Zeitlin.
Thank you, Anna Radunsky and Sasha Radunsky.
Thank you, all, for the beautiful drawings and
paintings you generously gave to me for this book. —V. R.

The publisher wishes to acknowledge the help and support
of Nora Guthrie and Judy Bell; and Bing Broderick of
Rounder Records in the publication of this book.

Thank you, Paul Colin, for your help in bringing
this book to a glorious conclusion. —V. R.

ZIPPY

ZIPPY'S SUN, TIGER AND LION